This story is based on the descriptively enhanced screenplay
developed for "The Animated Stories from the New Testament" video series.
Scripture references have been provided for those readers who
would like to read the story as it is related in the Bible.

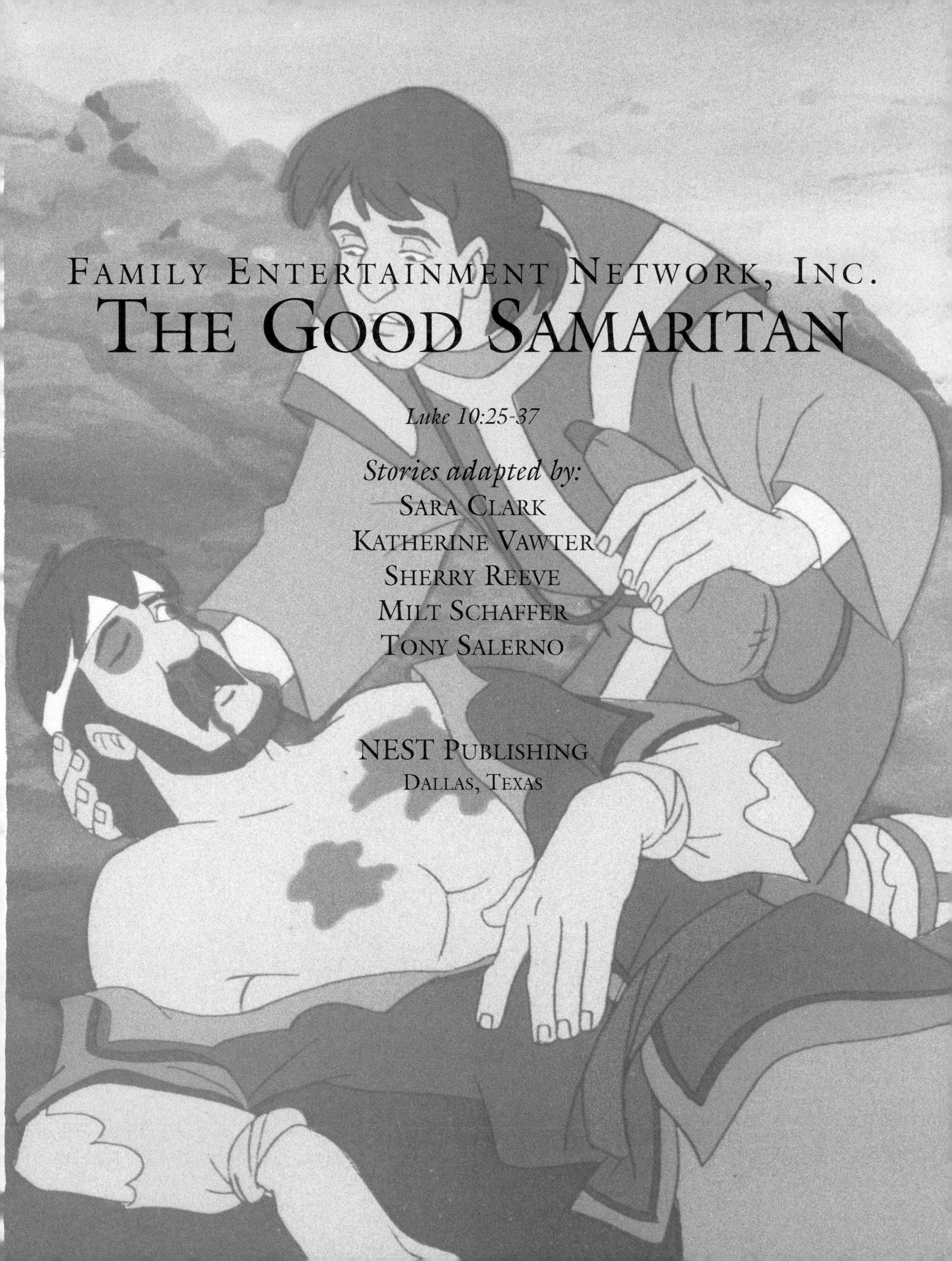

Family Entertainment Network, Inc.
The Good Samaritan

Luke 10:25-37

Stories adapted by:
Sara Clark
Katherine Vawter
Sherry Reeve
Milt Schaffer
Tony Salerno

NEST Publishing
Dallas, Texas

The house in Judea was plain with dirt floors. The walls were made of clay. The tables and chairs were of ordinary wood. The cups and dishes were not silver or gold. They were just common pottery. The men who had gathered in this humble place were very excited. One might have thought they had come to a palace to visit a king. They had. They had come to visit Jesus - Prince of Peace, King of Kings.

Jesus was surrounded by his disciples. Standing nearby were wealthy merchants, priests, teachers, holy men, and lawyers. They had come to hear Him speak. They had come to ask Him questions. They had even come to challenge His teaching.

Jesus spoke to the group. "How blessed you are. For many prophets and kings have desired to see the things that you have seen and to hear the things that you have heard, but have seen and heard them not."

Jesus was speaking of heaven, the kingdom of God, and eternal life.

2

He was interrupted by a man who did not believe that Jesus was the Messiah. He wanted to trick Jesus so he asked a question. "Excuse me, Master. But may I ask a question? What must I do to inherit eternal life?"

"You are a lawyer?" Jesus asked. The colorfully dressed man nodded yes. Then Jesus inquired, "What is written in the law? How do you read it?"

The lawyer answered. "It says 'Love the Lord your God, with all your heart, with all your soul, with all your strength, with all your mind, and love your neighbor as yourself.'"

Jesus said, "You have answered right. Do this and you will live."

Hoping to trick Jesus, the lawyer asked, "Ahhh ... but who is my neighbor?"

"I have listened," said Jesus. "Now would you listen?" Then Jesus told a story that would help the lawyer understand what it really means to be a neighbor.

There once was a friendly innkeeper named Gaal. One day he stood at his hearth. He was cooking a hearty meal for the tired travelers who were staying at his inn. His son, Josh, was a good boy. He liked to help his father. Gaal handed his son a bowl of soup. "It's for one of the men in the corner, Josh," Gaal said.

"Yes, Papa," said Josh. Then he took the bowl to a table where two hungry men sat.

One of the two men was a small, sly-looking man called Kish. He was counting some coins, "Sixteen, seventeen, eighteen, nineteen, twenty ..." He slowly stacked the coins one by one. But the coins all fell over when Josh startled him by saying, "Excuse me, sir, your soup."

Kish laughed, "Why, thank you little boy." And he patted Josh on the head.

The other man at the table was Nadab. Nadab was younger than Kish. He was a big man with more muscles than brains. Nadab also patted Josh on the head, "Yeah, uh ... thank you, little boy."

"Nadab, you fool!" shouted Kish. "He hasn't even brought you your bowl yet!"

"Oh ...," said Nadab. Then he pounded the table with his fist. "Well, where is it?" asked the angry Nadab.

Josh did not like these two strangers, but he was polite. "I'll bring it now, sir," he said.

When the boy was gone, Kish put more coins from his money bag onto the table. "Robbing is so much fun. It certainly pays well," he laughed.

"How much do I get, Kish?" Nadab asked.

"Well, now, let's divide this evenly," said Kish. Then he gave Nadab a single coin and put the rest in his own money bag. "There!" he said.

"Oh, thanks, Kish," said Nadab. He didn't know that Kish had cheated him. "Now I'm as rich as you, right?"

"Right, right," Kish answered.

"When do we rob again?" asked Nadab.

"I have a new plan," said Kish. "From now on, we'll rob the travelers before they reach Jericho. That way we get all their gold before they've spent anything here at Gaal's inn."

"Can I still mash 'em?" asked Nadab. He was excited.

"That's your job, Nadab," Kish answered. "To mash them dead! A dead trader can't tell the soldiers who robbed him."

"How will I know when he's dead, Kish?" Nadab asked.

"When he stops moving, Nadab," said Kish. "You're so dumb!"

"I don't like it when you call me dumb!" shouted Nadab. He grabbed Kish by the collar and lifted him up out of his chair.

"Aaarrrgghhh!" choked Kish. "A slip of the tongue, Nadab. I meant to say delightful. You are so delightful."

Kish was lying. But Nadab believed that he was really sorry. Nadab dropped Kish back into his chair.

Finally, Gaal the innkeeper had heard enough from these two men. "Get out of my inn!" he shouted. "I won't have any thieves or robbers here. Run, Josh, and get the soldiers."

"Soldiers? No soldiers!" Kish begged. "We're going. We're leaving."

"But I didn't eat yet, Kish," said Nadab.

"We are going, Nadab," said Kish. He walked toward the door. "We don't want any trouble."

"But I'm hungry, Kish," said Nadab. "I want my dinner."

When the two thieves were gone, Josh turned to his father, "I was scared, Papa."

"They won't cause any harm here in Jericho, but I feel sorry for anyone traveling alone on the road from Jerusalem tomorrow," said the Innkeeper.

That same day, in the distant city of Jerusalem, a little girl named Rebecca watched her father, Ezra. He was preparing his herbs and spices to be sold in the marketplace. He also sold his spices to merchants and traders in far away cities.

"What are you grinding up today, Papa?" asked Rebecca.

Her father answered, "Basil, for the emperor's own kitchen." Ezra went to a shelf filled with herbs and spices. He took some peppercorns from a bag.

"Those are hot, black peppercorns from Java," said Rebecca.

"Very good, Rebecca," encouraged her father. "You are truly a spice merchant's daughter."

"I know all the spices," said Rebecca proudly. "Cumin and peppermint from India ... frankincense and sweet spices from Sa'aba ... red peppers like fire from Cathay.

Rebecca saw her little brother Aaron. He was standing on his tiptoes on a stool. His hand was in the sack of peppercorns. "Oh, no! Papa!" Rebecca shouted. "Aaron's playing in the black peppercorns from Java."

"Aaron!" said Ezra. He lifted his young son and put him down on the floor away from the hot spice.

But not before little Aaron had put some of the peppercorns into his mouth. He started crying, "Hot, hot, hot!"

"Quickly, Rebecca, get some water," instructed her father. While Ezra held Aaron, Rebecca washed the peppercorns from his mouth.

"Never, never eat spices, Aaron. Never!" warned Ezra.

"Never, never, never," repeated little Aaron.

It was then that Ezra's wife, Hanna, entered the room. "I packed everything for your journey, Ezra." she said. Then she noticed little Aaron covered with water and peppercorns.

Rebecca was quick to explain to her mother about Aaron and the peppercorns.

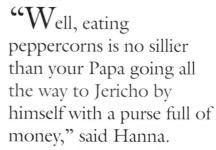

"Well, eating peppercorns is no sillier than your Papa going all the way to Jericho by himself with a purse full of money," said Hanna.

"This journey will make us rich, my love," Ezra replied.

"I'd rather be a poor Jewish wife than a rich widow," said Hanna.

Ezra hid his money bag inside his shirt. "There now," Ezra said. "No one will see I have any money, so they won't try to rob me."

15

Outside the doorway, Ezra kissed his wife. "Good-bye, now," he called to his family.

Rebecca ran to her father and cried, "Papa! Can I go with you?"

"You stay at home, Rebecca, and help your mother," said Ezra. He kissed her on the forehead. "By nightfall I'll be in Jericho at Gaal's Inn."

"Be careful, Ezra," begged his worried wife.

"Good-bye, Papa!" Rebecca called out. And Ezra, with his donkey, started down the road.

Meanwhile, in a place called Samaria, there lived a tall, handsome Samaritan named Caleb. He was also preparing for a journey.

"Are you sure you don't want a servant to take this horse to Moab?" asked Delsia, Caleb's worried mother.

"This stallion is the last part of my sister's dowry, Mother," answered Caleb. "I'll deliver it myself."

"Well, promise me you won't stop at Jerusalem," said Delsia.

"Don't worry, Mother," Caleb laughed. "I'll be in Jericho long before dark."

"God be with you, my son," said Delsia. And Caleb rode off toward Jericho.

In another town, not far away, a priest named Matthias had prepared for a journey. His journey would also take him on the road through Jericho.

"I'm ready, sir," said Matthias to an old priest.

"Good," the old priest replied. "Take this scroll to the synagogue in Damascus. Now, let nothing delay you."

"I won't stop for anything, sir. I'm on the Lord's business," said Matthias.

"You are a priest," said the old priest. "Everything you do is the Lord's business,"

"Oh yes, well ..." Matthias answered. "Farewell, sir. I will be in Jericho before nightfall." He got onto his donkey and rode off.

And in yet another town, a man named Jeshua prepared for his journey to Galilee.

"Now, remember, Jeshua," warned his brother. "You are a Levite. Don't touch anything unclean or you'll have to go through weeks of purification when you get back from Galilee."

"I just wish I could go straight to Capernaum instead of having to walk all the way around Samaria," Jeshua said.

"What?" shouted his brother. "You mean you'd walk through Samaria? That's such a vile place. You'd never get purified."

"But it's just so inconvenient having to go around by way of Jericho," Jeshua complained.

"Better that than having to deal with Samaritans!" warned his brother. "Remember that, Jeshua. Now be safe and don't dawdle along the way."

19

Meanwhile, back in Jerusalem, Ezra the spice merchant had reached the city gates.

"Good journey to you," said the guard at the gate.

"Thank you, sir," said Ezra.

At that moment, Caleb also arrived at the city gates. He was riding his sister's unruly stallion. He told the horse to settle down. Then he pulled on the reins tightly to keep the horse from crashing into Ezra's donkey. "Sorry," Caleb called to Ezra.

Ezra calmed his donkey and continued on his way.

The guard at the gate looked at Caleb and asked, "Who are you? What brings you to Jerusalem?"

"I just wanted to buy some food and drink before I go on to Moab," Caleb answered. "I'm from Samaria and I ..."

"A Samaritan!" shouted the guard. "I thought so."

"A Samaritan?" asked a man passing by.

"No Samaritans in Jerusalem!" angrily shouted another.

And another shouted at Caleb, "Go back to Samaria where you belong!"

An angry crowd gathered quickly. Some of them started to throw stones at Caleb. "We don't want your kind in Judea!" yelled a man in the crowd.

"Please stop!" Caleb cried in pain as the stones hit him. Caleb turned his horse to escape being hit by more stones.

A man shouted, "That's right. Run away, Samaritan. You coward!"

Matthias, the priest, and Jeshua, the Levite, arrived in Jerusalem just in time to see Caleb ride off on his horse. He was dodging stones being thrown by the angry crowd.

"What was all the disturbance?" Matthias asked his fellow traveler.

"They were shouting something about a Samaritan," said Jeshua.

"Those Samaritans!" said Matthias. "No doubt he tried to pick a fight."

"Why don't they just stay in Samaria?" said Jeshua.

"My thoughts exactly. Good day, friend," said the priest. And the two set off separately down the road to Jericho.

23

Not far away, the wicked Kish and Nadab walked along the dusty road between Jerusalem and Jericho. "Are we there yet, Kish?" the big man asked. "It's hot. I'm tired."

"Nadab, do you want to be a robber or not?" said Kish.

"Yes, Kish," Nadab answered.

"Then stop complaining," said Kish. He looked at the rocky hills on either side of the road. "This looks like a good place. Come on, Nadab. Climb up behind these rocks and we'll wait for the first traveler to come worthy of being robbed."

"Then can I mash him to bits, Kish?" Nadab asked as he climbed the steep rocks.

"Yes, Nadab. Then you can mash him to bits." Then Kish turned to look down at the road from their look-out point. "Yes, this is perfect," he said.

Not far away, Caleb had stopped to rest near a stream. He was battered and bruised from the rocks thrown at him. But he was more worried about his horse. He gently poured cool water on the stallion. "There. Does that feel better now?" he asked. The horse neighed to show that he enjoyed this kindness.

Caleb rubbed his own aches and bruises. "Ow! Maybe mother was right. Maybe all people do hate us Samaritans," Caleb said as he mounted his horse.

Close by, Kish and Nadab looked down from their ledge above the road. They were watching for any travelers on their way to Jericho. Before long the two sneaky thieves heard someone coming along the road. It was Ezra the spice merchant. His donkey had suddenly become stubborn.

"Whoa. Whoa, boy!" they heard Ezra say to his donkey. "What's wrong? Come on, now. We have to get to Jerico before dark."

Up on the ledge Kish laughed softly. "Oh good. Here comes one all alone. And on a donkey."

"A donkey?" Nadab asked. "Can I ride him, Kish?"

"You're too big. You'd crush it," said Kish. "I'll ride the donkey. Quiet, quiet now," Kish warned Nadab. Then the two men prepared for the attack. "Get above him! Ready ... ready ... mash him!"

27

Nadab jumped from behind the rocks onto Ezra. Kish shouted instructions. "Hit 'em again ... again ... and again! Good. Good!"

Nadab looked down at Ezra then said to Kish, "Oh, uh ... he's stopped moving, Kish."

"Good," said Kish. "Get his money bag."

Nadab grabbed a bag hanging from Ezra's belt. He opened it and looked inside. "It's empty, Kish!" he shouted.

But Kish was not fooled. He reached inside Ezra's shirt and snatched the purse hidden there. "They always have a purse around their neck," shouted Kish. The two men laughed as they counted the money.

Kish pointed to Ezra and said to Nadab, "now, get rid of the body." Nadab picked up Ezra and threw him off the side of the road. Kish rode off on Ezra's donkey.

When Nadab saw him he yelled. "Hey, Kish, wait for me!" And he ran to catch up.

A hot midday wind blew over Ezra's beaten body. Somehow, he had pulled himself up to the edge of the road.

He was lying there, moaning in pain, when Matthias, the priest, found him. "Poor man. If I wasn't on the Lord's business, I'd have time to stop," said Matthias.

"Help me ... please," Ezra weakly cried out.

"Oh, Lord. Please help this unfortunate man," Matthias prayed. And the priest went on his way to Jericho.

Not long afterward, Jeshua came walking along. He was nibbling on some nuts and berries. Ezra called out to Jeshua, "Please ... please."

Jeshua looked down. When he saw Ezra he was scared. He looked from side to side nervously. "You were robbed! And that means there are robbers around here," he said. Then he shouted so that any robbers might hear. "I'm a Levite! I don't have any money!"

Ezra was left, once again, lying alone at the edge of the road. There was no help in sight. He began to think that he would never make it home alive. He prayed, "Oh, Lord. Be merciful to my family when I am dead." Then he moaned and lay still.

Just then Caleb, the Samaritan, came riding along. He found Ezra lying among the rocks and sand. The young man slid off his horse and knelt beside the beaten man. "He's still breathing," he said. "He's alive! He's hurt bad. Who could have done such a thing?"

Caleb ripped off a piece of cloth from his own robe. He used it to wrap Ezra's bleeding head.

"Ohhh ...," Ezra moaned weakly. "Thank you, sir. Thank you for stopping ..."

"This will sting, poor man," Caleb said. "But these cuts need cleansing." Then he gently covered Ezra's wounds with oil and wine.

"Here, drink this," said the Samaritan. He lifted Ezra's head and poured some water slowly into his dry mouth.

Ezra looked up. "Robbers ... they ... come back ...," he said weakly.

"That's right," Caleb agreed. "They might come back. So, we have to get you to Jericho." Then Caleb carefully lifted Ezra onto his horse.

35

Meanwhile, down the road in Jericho, Jeshua and Matthias sat together at Gaal's inn. They were both eating some of Gaal's soup.

"Yumm ...," said Jeshua. "Very good food here."

"Even if the food were terrible," Matthias replied, "I'd be grateful to have it. The road to Jericho is very dangerous."

Suddenly the door flew open and Caleb entered. He carried Ezra into the safety of the inn. "Innkeeper!" he called out. "Help me! This man is badly hurt."

"Lay him here," said Gaal quickly clearing a table. Then he motioned to his son for help. "Josh! Quickly! Fetch hot water and clean rags!"

"All I had was the hem of my own robe," said Caleb.

"You did fine, young man," said Gaal. "But so dangerous! The robbers might have attacked you while you bandaged him."

"I couldn't very well leave him there to die, could I?" asked Caleb.

The innkeeper shook his head. He pointed toward Jeshua and Matthias now enjoying their soup. "Those two men came along the Jericho road just an hour ago," he said. Jeshua and Matthias got up and walked to the table where Ezra lay.

Caleb said to the two men. "Well, he must have been robbed and beaten right after you passed then. I thought at first he was dead."

"I think he'll live, thanks to you, sir," said Gaal to Caleb. "Where did you travel from?"

"Samaria," answered Caleb.

"Samaria!" said Matthias.

"A Samaritan!" spat Jeshua. "Ugh!"

The innkeeper ignored these rude remarks. He called to his son, "Josh, make a bed for this poor man there by the fire so he won't get a chill."

"Yes, Papa," said Josh obediently. The boy unrolled a soft mat. And Caleb carefully laid Ezra down next to the warm fireplace.

"He's sure lucky you came along," said Josh to Caleb.

"No, I just did what anyone would do," said Caleb humbly.

The priest and the Levite looked angrily at Caleb. They hated him because he was a Samaritan.

When Ezra awoke the next morning, he was strong enough to sit up. He even sipped a bowl of warm soup Josh brought to him.

Suddenly, the door of the inn flew open. Ezra and the boy looked to see a palace guard with Kish and Nadab. "Sir, are these the men?" the guard asked.

In a weak voice Ezra answered, "Yes, those are the men."

"You ... you liar," shouted the evil Kish.

Nadab spoke up proudly, "I mashed him ten times!" Then he pointed to Kish. "Just like you said, Kish!"

"Ohhhhh!" gasped Kish. "You're so dumb! Aaugh!"

"Come along," the guard commanded. Then he took his two prisoners out of the inn.

Josh turned to Ezra. He said happily, "Well, they won't be robbing anymore."

Just then Jeshua, the Levite, entered the room. He handed Gaal money for his room and board. "Very good food," the Levite said, "but ... Samaritans."

Matthias, following him, agreed, "Yes, you ought to be more careful about whom you allow to stay in your inn."

It was then that Caleb
entered the room. He
went over and placed his
hand softly on Ezra's
shoulder. "How are you
feeling this morning?" the
Samaritan asked.

"Much better, kind sir,"
answered Ezra. His eyes
were filled with
thankfulness.

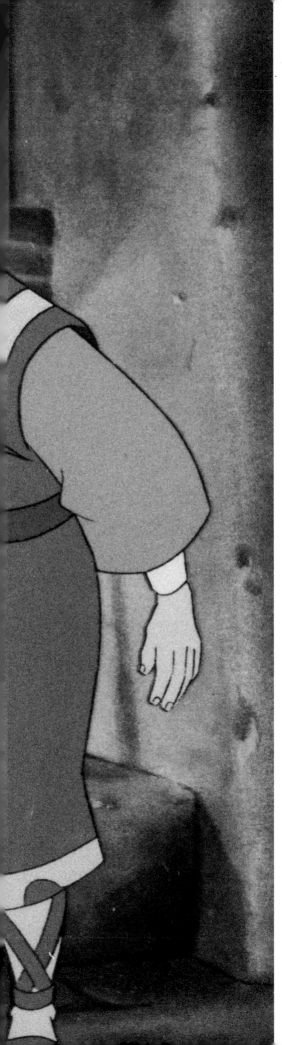

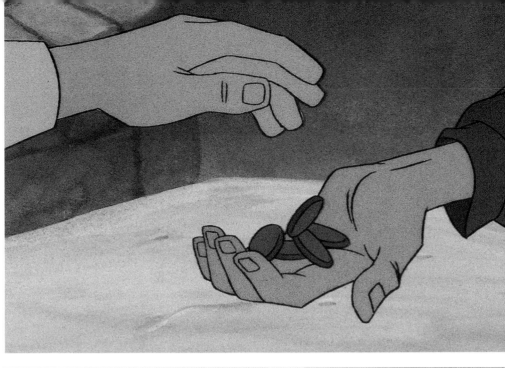

"Oh good, I'm glad," said Caleb as he turned to Gaal. "Here's the money for my lodging, sir. And here's payment for this man's bed and food until he's better. And, if it isn't enough, well, I'll pay you more when I come back through here after my business is done in Moab."

"Thank you, sir," said the innkeeper. "I hope my son grows up to be as kind as you."

"I just did what anyone would do," said Caleb. Then he opened the door to leave. "Peace be unto you."

"And peace be with you!" Josh eagerly called to the good Samaritan. The door closed and the Samaritan was gone.

43

W hen Jesus had finished the story of the Good Samaritan, He turned to the lawyer. "Now which of them was neighbor to the man who fell among thieves?" He asked.
"It was the Samaritan," said the lawyer. "It was the one who showed mercy on him."
"Go and do likewise," said Jesus to the lawyer. "Then you, too, will be blessed of God."

THE END

MY HANDS

Lyrics by
CAROL LYNN PEARSON

Music by
LEX DE AZEVEDO
Arranged by PAUL FISCHER